Curly is not sure what that means, but she trusts her dad to do what's best. So instead of starting to worry, Curly helps Dad set up camp.

By the time they are finished, the sun has already begun to set. Dad gathers wood so they can start a campfire to keep them warm all night. Curly helps organize the wood into a neat pile.

Shortly after nightfall, the fire is lit. Curly and Dad are both extremely hungry. All that remains of their food is a bag of marshmallows. As they roast them over the fire, Dad promises, "I will gather proper food for breakfast."

Lying down that night, Curly and Dad gaze at the beauty of the night sky, full of stars, galaxies, and nebulae. They even see a few shooting stars. They make a wish on each one!

Curly and Dad sleep soundly all night, even with all the nighttime noises in the forest. They have chosen a perfect campsite—near a little stream, and hidden from sight.

As the sun rises, Curly opens her eyes. Where is Dad? Curly calls out to him. Then out he walks from behind a clump of trees with something dangling from his mouth.

Dad stops in front of Curly, opens his beak, and a bunch of worms fall to the ground. "Breakfast is served!" he says. Curly is not sure what to think. Worms? She was hoping for a pile of chocolate donuts or a big, juicy hamburger.

Dad sees the look on her face. He says, "Before discovering the awesomeness of dumpsters, crows used to eat things like worms." Reluctantly, Curly tries one. Dad is right! The worm tastes delicious!

"Let's take a hike up the mountain," Dad says. "You can hold the compass." They navigate through the forest until they reach the base of a tall mountain.

On the way up, Curly remarks on the beauty of nature. "I never saw so many trees and flowers." The amazing landscape looks like something you would see in a movie.

When Curly complains about being thirsty, Dad teaches her how to find water. He leads her through the woods until they find a cool, refreshing stream.

Dad also shows Curly new places to find food——no, not in a dumpster! They look on the bark of the trees, among the tall grass, and even in the soil. They feast on more worms, some insects, and a few wild berries.

Curly is so thankful that her dad is teaching her these survival techniques. If Dad didn't know how to gather food or make a campfire, they would be cold and hungry.

Their final night under the stars is beautiful. A full moon lights up the night. Curly is surprised at how much light the full moon provides. "It's almost as bright as the day!" she exclaims.

In the morning, they pack up their belongings. "Be sure to clean up the campsite," Dad says, "because that's the responsible thing to do. No one wants trash polluting the wilderness!"

Curly feels a little sad to be going home. Camping is so much fun that she doesn't want to leave. But her family probably misses her, and she definitely misses them.

The second she gets home, Curly runs to her mom to tell her about the trip! She chatters so fast that Mom can barely follow what she's saying! But one thing is for sure: Camping is amazing!

# THE END

# About the Author

Nicholas Aragon is the author of the Curly Crow children's book series. Inspired by his mother Barb Keady (1959-2017), Nicholas started Curly Crow LLC with a mission to inspire and heal the human spirit through art. A native New Mexican, Nicholas enjoys fishing and spending time outdoors with his amazing wife and two beautiful daughters.

Before he started writing children's books, Nicholas got a graduate degree in Higher Education Administration from NMSU. After that, just to shake things up, he started an online business where he sells Curly Crow Art, Apparel, and Children's Books. In addition to writing amazing children's books, Nicholas works full time as a Higher Education Administrator where he satisfies his passion to help change lives one student at a time.

If you want to know when the next Curly Crow book will come out, please visit our website at, https://www.curlycrow.com/book-shop/ where you can sign up to receive an email when he has his next release.

Made in the USA
Middletown, DE
29 August 2023

36999119R00020